MARVEL

MARVEL ACTION

BLACK PANTHER

STORMY WEATHER

Marvel Publishing:

Jeff Youngquist: VP Production & Special Projects
Caitlin O'Connell: Assistant Editor, Special Projects
Sven Larsen: Director, Licensed Publishing
David Gabriel: SVP Print, Sales & Marketing
C.B. Cebulski: Editor In Chief
Joe Quesada: Chief Creative Officer
Dan Buckley: President, Marvel Entertainment
Alan Fine: Executive Producer

IDW Publishing:

Chris Ryall, President and Publisher/CCO
John Barber, Editor-In-Chief
Cara Morrison, Chief Financial Officer
Matt Ruzicka, Chief Accounting Officer
David Hedgecock, Associate Publisher
Jerry Bennington, VP of New Product Development
Lorelei Bunjes, VP of Digital Services
Justin Eisinger, Editorial Director, Graphic Novels & Collections
Eric Moss, Senior Director, Licensing and Business Development

Ted Adams and Robbie Robbins, IDW Founders

Collection Edits
JUSTIN EISINGER
and ALONZO SIMON

Production Assistance
SHAWN LEE

Cover Art by
PAULINA GANUCHEAU

ISBN: 978-1-68405-517-3   22 21 20 19   1 2 3 4

Special thanks: Wil Moss

MARVEL ACTION: BLACK PANTHER: STORMY WEATHER (BOOK 1). DECEMBER 2019. FIRST PRINTING.

Originally published as MARVEL ACTION: BLACK PANTHER issues #1–3.

For international rights, contact licensing@idwpublishing.com

MARVEL

MARVEL ACTION

BLACK PANTHER

STORMY WEATHER

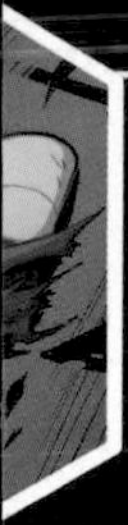

WRITTEN BY KYLE BAKER

ART BY JUAN SAMU

COLORS BY DAVID GARCIA CRUZ

LETTERS BY TOM B. LONG & SHAWN LEE

ASSISTANT EDITOR ANNI PERHEENTUPA

ASSOCIATE EDITORS ELIZABETH BREI & CHASE MAROTZ

EDITOR DENTON J. TIPTON

EDITOR-IN-CHIEF JOHN BARBER

BLACK PANTHER CREATED BY STAN LEE & JACK KIRBY

ART BY: JUAN SAMU
COLORS BY: DAVID GARCIA CRUZ

THE BLACK PANTHER HAS BESTED MANY ADVERSARIES IN THE PAST, BUT EVEN HE CANNOT WITHSTAND THE FULL FURY OF HIS MIGHTIEST OPPONENT YET: MOTHER NATURE!
THE LITTLE THINGS

Wakanda.
COUGH COUGH
COUGH COUGH COUGH
MOOOOOOO

AAAAH!

"I'M SORRY, YOUR HIGHNESS. WE EXPECTED MORE PEOPLE."
IT'S THE HEAT. I DON'T BLAME ANYONE.
YOU KNOW BLACK ABSORBS HEAT, RIGHT?
YOU KNOW VIBRANIUM ABSORBS ENERGY, RIGHT, SHURI? HEAT IS ENERGY.
WOW. YOU DID NOT JUST EXPLAIN MY OWN DESIGN TO ME, T'CHALLA.
HE DID, SWEET-HEART.
YOU DID.
WELL, SHE STARTED IT, MOTHER!
I COULD MAKE YOU THAT SAME OUTFIT IN DAY-GLO YELLOW OR GREEN.
THE PURPLE PANTHER! THAT'S AN AWESOME NAME!
SHURI, STOP TEASING YOUR BROTHER.
THE SILVER PANTHER! REFLECTIVE SURFACES REPEL HEAT!
SERIOUSLY?
ARE YOU SERIOUSLY ASKING "SERIOUSLY?"
THE SEQUINED PANTHER?

I THANK YOU ALL FOR COMING OUT TODAY. AS I GAZE OUT UPON THE MULTITUDE OF FACES...
COUGH COUGH
WAKANDA'S TRUE WEALTH IS NOT VIBRANIUM. WAKANDA'S REAL TREASURE IS ITS PEOPLE.
WAKANDA IS NOT JUST ITS KING. WAKANDA IS EVERYONE. EVERYONE IS VALUABLE. THE YOUNG, THE OLD, THE STRONG, THE WEAK. ALL ARE RESPECTED AND PROTECTED.
THIS YEAR HAS BROUGHT MORE PROSPERITY THAN EVER. VIBRANIUM PRODUCTION HAS TRIPLED! FOR THAT, WE HAVE TO THANK THE NEW CHIEF OF MINING, MR. MCHEZAJI.
IT'S GOOD TO FINALLY MEET YOU. EVERY WAKANDAN OWES YOU A DEBT OF THANKS.

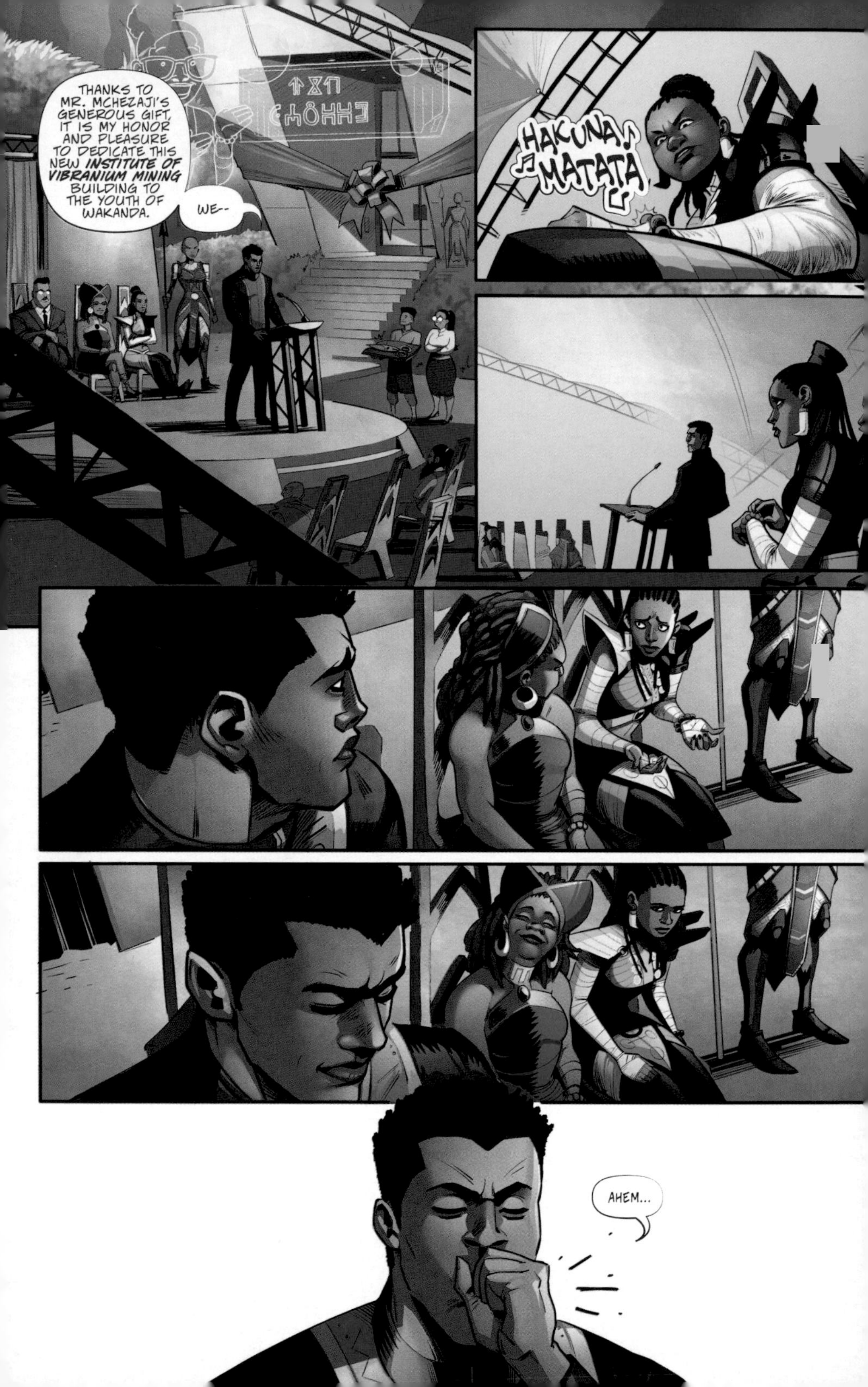
THANKS TO MR. MCHEZAJI'S GENEROUS GIFT, IT IS MY HONOR AND PLEASURE TO DEDICATE THIS NEW INSTITUTE OF VIBRANIUM MINING BUILDING TO THE YOUTH OF WAKANDA.
WE--
HAKUNA MATATA
AHEM...

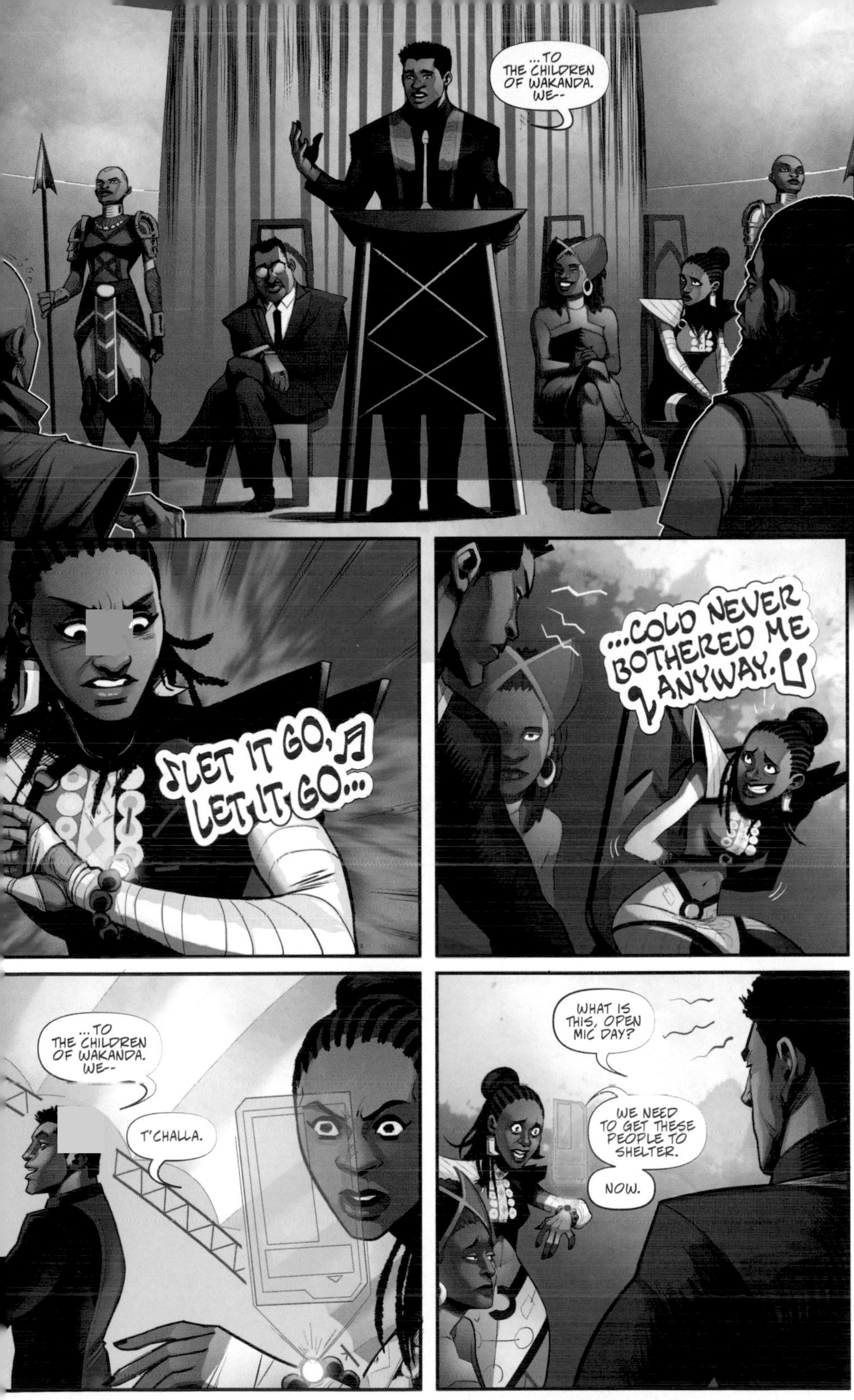
...TO THE CHILDREN OF WAKANDA. WE--
LET IT GO, LET IT GO...
...COLD NEVER BOTHERED ME ANYWAY.
...TO THE CHILDREN OF WAKANDA. WE--
T'CHALLA.
WHAT IS THIS, OPEN MIC DAY?
WE NEED TO GET THESE PEOPLE TO SHELTER.
NOW.

SUCH A BUMPY FLIGHT.
I KNOW, RIGHT?
THIS IS YOUR CAPTAIN. WE SEEM TO HAVE SOME UNEXPECTED TURBULENCE.
PLEASE RETURN TO YOUR SEATS AND FASTEN YOUR--
BOOM

GET INSIDE!
COME BACK!
BARKY! WHERE'S BARKY?
I NEED BARKY!

WHERE ARE YOU, BARKY?!
ARF! ARF! ARF!
ARF! ARF!
BARKY!
WHOOOOSH

K-KRACK
WHOOSH
ZING
HURRY, MY KING!
IT'S RIGHT BEHIND YOU!

SLAM
YOU MADE IT!
THAK
THAK
THAK
THANK YOU, YOUR HIGHNESS. THANK YOU SO MUCH.
MAMA!

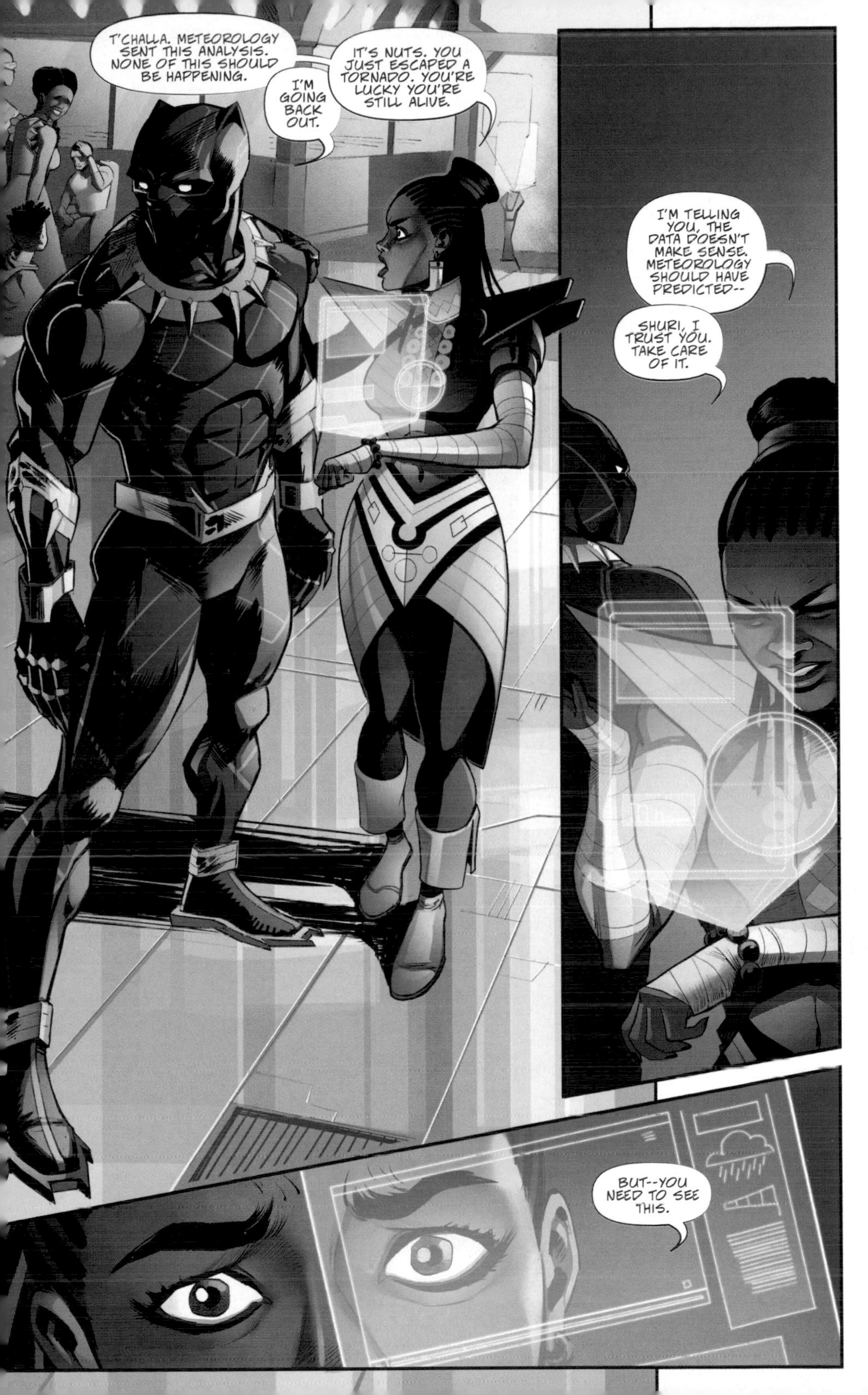
T'CHALLA. METEOROLOGY SENT THIS ANALYSIS. NONE OF THIS SHOULD BE HAPPENING.
I'M GOING BACK OUT.
IT'S NUTS. YOU JUST ESCAPED A TORNADO. YOU'RE LUCKY YOU'RE STILL ALIVE.
I'M TELLING YOU, THE DATA DOESN'T MAKE SENSE. METEOROLOGY SHOULD HAVE PREDICTED--
SHURI, I TRUST YOU. TAKE CARE OF IT.
BUT--YOU NEED TO SEE THIS.

THAT JET IS GOING DOWN AND HEADING THIS WAY!
AND IT HAS ***INCREDIBLE*** MASS. YOU KNOW WHAT THAT CALLS FOR, BROTHER.
CRACK
THIS IS YOUR CAPTAIN.
PREPARE FOR A CRASH LANDING.
AAAAA!
EEEEE!
WAAAAAH!

WHAM
UNH!
SKRRRUUNCH

ARE WE IN THE AFTERWORLD?
I HOPE NOT. IT'S VERY HOT HERE.
SHURI, THE TORNADO HAS DISPERSED! DID T'CHALLA DO THAT, TOO?
DON'T BE RIDICULOUS, OKOYE!
IT WAS THE HULKBUSTER ARMOR. IT ABSORBS ENERGY. KINETIC ENERGY, IN THIS CASE.
BUT IT DOESN'T DO ANYTHING FOR FALLING DEBRIS, SO EYES ON THE SKIES...
IS EVERYONE OKAY?
YES. THANK YOU, MY KING.
JUST DOING MY JOB. STAY IN SCHOOL, KIDS.

NO! THE NANITES ARE GLOWING. HE'S HOLDING ALL THE KINETIC ENERGY FROM THE IMPACT AND TORNADO! ONE HUG WILL BLOW YOUR ARMS OFF! MATTER OF FACT, EVERYBODY GET AWAY FROM HIM!
SHOO! GO!
YOU'VE GOT TO REDISTRIBUTE THAT ENERGY, T'CHALLA!
PREFERABLY HARMLESSLY.
WHAMO
I HOPE THAT RHINO KNOWS I SAVED HIS LIFE.

NEWS
EVERYONE REQUIRING MEDICAL ATTENTION AFTER THE TORNADO THIS MORNING HAS BEEN SEEN TO--
WHAT HAPPENED TO THIS POOR BULL?
HEATWAVE AND EPIDEMIC IN THE WESTERN FOREST. ABOUT HALF OUR FOOD SUPPLY IS AT RISK.
FIRES ARE FOLLOWED BY MUDSLIDES. DON'T GET ME STARTED ON AIR QUALITY.
WE STILL CAN'T GET A HANDLE ON THIS HEAT. AND IT SMELLS LIKE HOT COW IN HERE.
THE WEATHER IS SPECIFIC TO WAKANDA. OUTSIDE OUR BORDERS, WE SEE AN ENTIRELY DIFFERENT WEATHER SYSTEM.
IT'S LIKE THE WEATHER IS TARGETING WAKANDA.
PEOPLE ARE DYING, T'CHALLA.
THEN WE'D BETTER FIND OUT WHAT'S GOING ON.
YOU AND YOUR SCIENTISTS SHOULD GET TO WORK--UPDATE ME AS SOON AS YOU HAVE NEWS.
WHAT'S DIFFERENT...? WHAT'S DIFFERENT...?
WHAT'S NEW...?

WOOOOOO
"FOUR TIMES AS MUCH VIBRANIUM PRODUCED TODAY."
"GOOD. I WANT EVERYONE TO ENJOY THIS."
SKATE
"I DON'T KNOW HOW YOU DO IT..."

...BUT I'M GOING OUT TO BUY A BOAT. YOU WANT A BOAT?
I'M GOOD, DARLING, THANKS.
I'M GETTING TWO BOATS SO I CAN CRASH THEM INTO EACH OTHER.
REMEMBER, WHEN I WIN, WE ALL WIN. REMEMBER.
WELL, NOT ALL OF US.

ART BY: ELSA CHARRETIER
COLORS BY: SARAH STERN

ART BY: JUAN SAMU
COLORS BY: DAVID GARCIA CRUZ

MUDSLIDES IN THE SOUTH, DROUGHT IN THE NORTH. THE STORMS DOWNWIND ONLY HELPED SPREAD THE WILDFIRES.
NOW FOR THE BAD NEWS...

...I'VE ANALYZED THE LIVESTOCK THAT THE AGRICULTURE MINISTRY SHIPPED HERE--IT'S AN EPIDEMIC. MALARIA. AND NOT ORDINARY MALARIA.
HAAA
HHHHHH!
COULD YOU REPEAT THAT?
THERE'S SCREAMING HERE.
WAIT, WHERE ARE YOU? YOU'RE NOT SENDING VIDEO, JUST AUDIO.
I'M AT WORK. PLEASE CONTINUE.
INCOMING: T'CHALLA
CLIMATIC EVENTS
AAAAAAAAAAHHHHHHH
WHAT'S THAT NOISE? T'CHALLA, ARE YOU IN THE FIRE? WHY DID YOU TAKE THIS CALL? I'LL CALL BACK.
NO, I NEED TO HEAR YOUR BRIEFING.
YOU NEED TO DEAL WITH WHAT'S IN FRONT OF YOU. YOU CAN'T DO EVERYTHING AND BE EVERYWHERE.
BE A LEADER, NOT A RULER. I'LL HANDLE THIS HERE.
OH, I'VE GOT ANOTHER CALL. LET ME TAKE THIS. I'M HANGING UP. YOU NEED TO FOCUS. BYE.
SHURI! SHURI? HELLO?
KROOM

--SITUATION IS CRITICAL.
TIME IS RUNNING OUT.
DOCTOR, THE CURES HAVE BEEN GENERATED AND ARE READY TO SHIP. I'M JUST WAITING FOR MY SECURITY ESCORT TO GET BACK.
OUR FORCES ARE STRETCHED THIN RIGHT NOW FIGHTING FIRES AND TORNADOES, BUT WE SHOULD HAVE WHEELS UP IN ABOUT THREE HOURS.
SOME OF US DON'T HAVE THREE HOURS. YOU KNOW THAT INFANTS AND THE ELDERLY FACE THE GREATEST RISK. PLEASE HURRY.
I-I'LL SEE WHAT I CAN DO.
EEEEEEEEE!!
WE'LL BE OKAY, LITTLE ONE. I PROMISE. DON'T WORRY.
COMPUTER. I NEED A RIDE.

SEE? EVERYTHING'S FINE. WE HAVE IT UNDER CONTROL.
RING
INCOMING MESSAGE FROM THE QUEEN MOTHER.
CAN I KEEP THE MASK?
MOTHER, I'M IN A LIFE-THREATENING CRISIS. CAN I CALL YOU BACK?
T'CHALLA I CAN'T REACH SH SHE'S NO ANSWERI MY CALL-
"SHURI'S BUSY. BETWEEN THE WEATHER AND THE--"

GAP!
--MALARIA. SHE TOLD ME.
WOOSSH!
YOU SAID YOU COULDN'T REACH HER.
THE SECOND TIME. WHEN I CALLED BACK. THE FIRST TIME, SHE SAID SHE WAS BUSY.
I HAVE TO GO, MOTHER. CALL SHURI BACK, LEAVE A MESSAGE.
I KNOW THERE IS A LOT GOING ON, BUT YOU NEED TO BE THERE FOR YOUR FAMILY, TOO.
OKAY, MOTHER...

...YOU'RE RIGHT. I'M SORRY. I'LL CALL HER AS SOON AS I CAN.
WTV
SHURI'S HEADED TO THE FARMLANDS. I WANT YOU TO GO INSTEAD.
BUT SHURI'S GOT THINGS UNDER CONTROL. I'LL DO MORE GOOD HERE.
T'CHALLA. SHURI IS GOING TO PIRANHA COVE...
"...REMEMBER WHAT HAPPENED LAST TIME?"
WAIT!

ASCENT INITIATED.
I HEARD YOU WERE GOING TO THE COVE AND THOUGHT YOU MIGHT WANT ME TO GO INSTEAD.
YOU MEAN MOTHER SENT YOU. WHAT AM I, A BABY? THE COVE WAS A LONG TIME AGO.
OKAY.
BUT YOU'RE HERE NOW, SO YOU CAN HELP WITH THE MISSION. IT'S ALL IN THESE CANNISTERS. ONE'S THE CURE, ONE'S THE VACCINE...
WHAT'S IN THE THIRD CAN?
MOSQUITO BAIT!
MOSQUITO BAIT? IT'S NOT BLOOD, IS IT? *EW!*

SOMETHING EVEN BETTER! MOSQUITOES CHOOSE THEIR VICTIMS BY SMELL.
YEAH?
THEY LIKE THE SMELL OF CHOLESTEROL, FOLIC ACID, CERTAIN BACTERIA, SKIN LOTIONS, PERFUME, AND OCTENOL--A CHEMICAL RELEASED IN SWEAT. DON'T OPEN THAT.
UGH! EW!
YOU COULD HAVE USED PERFUME AND YOU CHOSE SWEAT?
YUCK!
LIKE I'M GOING TO WASTE GOOD PERFUME ON INSECTS--THAT WE'RE GOING TO DESTROY?
DESTROY HOW?
A MOSQUITO TRAP. INDUSTRIAL SIZED.
WE'RE GOING TO KILL EVERY MOSQUITO IN WAKANDA.
BE CAREFUL WITH THAT. IT'S 46 MILLION YEARS OLD.

SINCE THE NEW CEO MCHEZAJI WAS APPOINTED, THE MINES HAVE QUADRUPLED PRODUCTION IN JUST ONE MONTH! AND WHAT'S GOOD FOR VIBRANIUM IS GOOD FOR WAKANDA!
WTV
FINANCIAL NEWS
Mchezaji new CEO
PAUSED
FINANCIAL NEWS
Mchezaji new CEO
--EXTREME WEATHER HAS INCREASED IN FREQUENCY AND INTENSITY FOR TWO MONTHS, EXTENDING THE LIFE CYCLE OF INSECTS THAT NORMALLY DIE AT COLDER TEMPERATURES. WE NEED TO--
!
INCOMING CALL FROM OKOYE
YOU'D BETTER ANSWER.
HELLO? MOTHER!

OKOYE
AM I KEEPING YOU FROM THE FINANCE NEWS?
WHAT? NO, THAT'S WEATHER DATA FROM THE LAB. STILL TRYING TO MAKE SENSE OF THE CLIMATE. WOULD YOU LIKE TO SPEAK TO T'CHALLA? HE'S GOT NOTHING TO DO.
SHURI
HE'S THERE? GOOD. I WAS WORRIED HE'D MISS THE FLIGHT.
WELL, I HATE TO KEEP YOU, SO I'LL LET YOU GO.
?
THERE'S SOMETHING ELSE NOW!
?
MA, I LOVE YOU, BUT I'VE GOT TO SAVE SOME LIVES RIGHT NOW. I'LL CALL YOU BACK.
FINANCIAL NEWS
SHURI... SHURI? HELLO?

"THAT IS A WEIRD COINCIDENCE."
NO SUCH THING. EVERY WEATHER DISASTER HAS CORRESPONDED EXACTLY WITH A SPIKE IN VIBRANIUM PRODUCTION. EXACTLY.
IF THAT WERE TRUE, MAYBE WE SHOULD PRAY FOR RAIN. WHAT'S GOOD FOR VIBRANIUM IS GOOD FOR WAKANDA.
AT WHAT COST?
MORE HOMES ARE BEING BUILT, MORE JOBS ARE BEING CREATED, RETAIL SALES ARE UP. I'M SURE NONE OF US WANT TO SEE THAT END.
WHO ELSE KNOWS ABOUT THIS?
I TRIED TO TELL SHURI, BUT... YOU KNOW CHILDREN. THEY THINK MY GENERATION DOESN'T KNOW ANYTHING.
SO NOBODY ELSE KNOWS.
YOU'RE THE FIRST. WHAT DO YOU THINK IT MEANS?
HAVE YOU EATEN? I'LL ORDER SOMETHING UP.

TURBULENCE AHEAD.
I DON'T LIKE THE LOOK OF THOSE CLOUDS. NOT WITH THIS HEAT. THIS IS A HURRICANE WAITING TO HAPPEN. OKAY, COMPUTER-- FLY LOWER.
INITIATING DESCENT FROM 30,000 FEET.
YOU THINK THERE'S ANOTHER STORM COMING?
I WOULDN'T WORRY. THERE'S BEEN A DROUGHT THERE FOR MONTHS. IF ANYTHING, I'D WORRY MORE ABOUT DUST STORMS GUMMING UP THE TURBINES.
DUST STORM STRAIGHT AHEAD.
WE'LL BE FINE. NO DUST STORM EVER REACHES ABOVE 20,000 FEET.
LEVELING OFF. 18,000 FEET.
HONESTLY, THEY RARELY REACH EVEN 17,000.
THWAM
TURBINE FAILURE. WARNING. TURBINE FAILURE.
SEATBELTS, PEOPLE! WE'RE GOING DOWN!
ARE YOU INSANE? WE'VE GOT TO GET OUT!
REALLY? YOU'RE GOING TO PARACHUTE INTO A 20,000-FOOT DUST STORM? THINK THAT ONE THROUGH. HOW'S THAT DECISION GOING TO PLAY OUT?
DON'T OPEN THAT DOOR!

WHOOOOOSH
PRESSURE COMPROMISED! EJECTION SEATS ACTIVATED!
AAAAAHHHHH!
NO!
THOOM
HUH. WHAT DO YOU KNOW? WE GOT EJECTED RIGHT OUT OF THE STORM.
DEPLOYING PARACHUTES.
COMPUTER! NO!
COMPUTER! CUT THE CHUTES!
WHAT?!
EEEEEEEEEE!
WHEW! THAT WAS A CLOSE ONE!
ALTITUDE: 17,000 FEET AND FALLING.
RIGHT. STILL A CLOSE ONE. THINK, SHURI!

I'M REALLY SORRY YOU FIGURED THIS OUT, QUEEN RAMONDA. I HAD HOPED TO WATCH SECRETLY AS WAKANDA SLOWLY CRUMBLED.
I WANTED TO SEE YOU WONDER WHAT HAD GONE WRONG, NEVER SUSPECTING FOR A MOMENT IT WAS ONE OF YOUR TRUSTED INNER CIRCLE.
"TRUSTED INNER CIRCLE" MIGHT BE STRETCHING IT.
NOW I'LL HAVE TO STEP UP THE TIMELINE SOMEWHAT. TAKE HER TO THE DUNGEON.
OF COURSE YOU HAVE A DUNGEON.
YOU CAN'T WIN THIS!
THANK YOUR MAKER I NEED YOU ALIVE. ATTACK!

THERE'S SOMETHING ON YOUR FACE.
POW
GOT IT FOR YOU.
BONK
YOU THINK I'M SCARED OF YOU?
YOU HAVE NO IDEA WHAT YOU'RE DEALING WITH!
?!

NOT LIKE THIS! NOT LIKE THIS!
ANY TIME NOW, SHURI.
PIRANHA COVE.
SHURI!
RIGHT.

WELL, THIS NET IS MEANT TO CATCH BUGS...
...BUT IT SHOULD HOLD UP...
...FOR AIRBORNE MAMMALS.
WHUMP
WHUMP
OH, WONDERFUL EARTH. I THOUGHT I'D NEVER SEE YOU AGAIN. LET US NEVER BE APART.
OKAY, LET'S FIND THE SHIP.
WHAT ABOUT CREWMAN LEZAR?

HE'S ON HIS OWN FOR NOW. WE NEED THE SHIP FOR SHELTER.
NO, WE NEED TO RECOVER THE MEDICINE.
HEY, LOOK AT THIS!
ISN'T IT ADORABLE?
NO! GET AWAY FROM IT!
IT'S JUST A BABY. IT CAN'T HURT ANYONE.
NO, BUT--
ROAARRRR
--BABIES HAVE MOTHERS.

ROARRRR
RUN!
RING
INCOMING CALL FROM QUEEN RAMONDA.
NOT ME. I GOT THE LAST ONE.

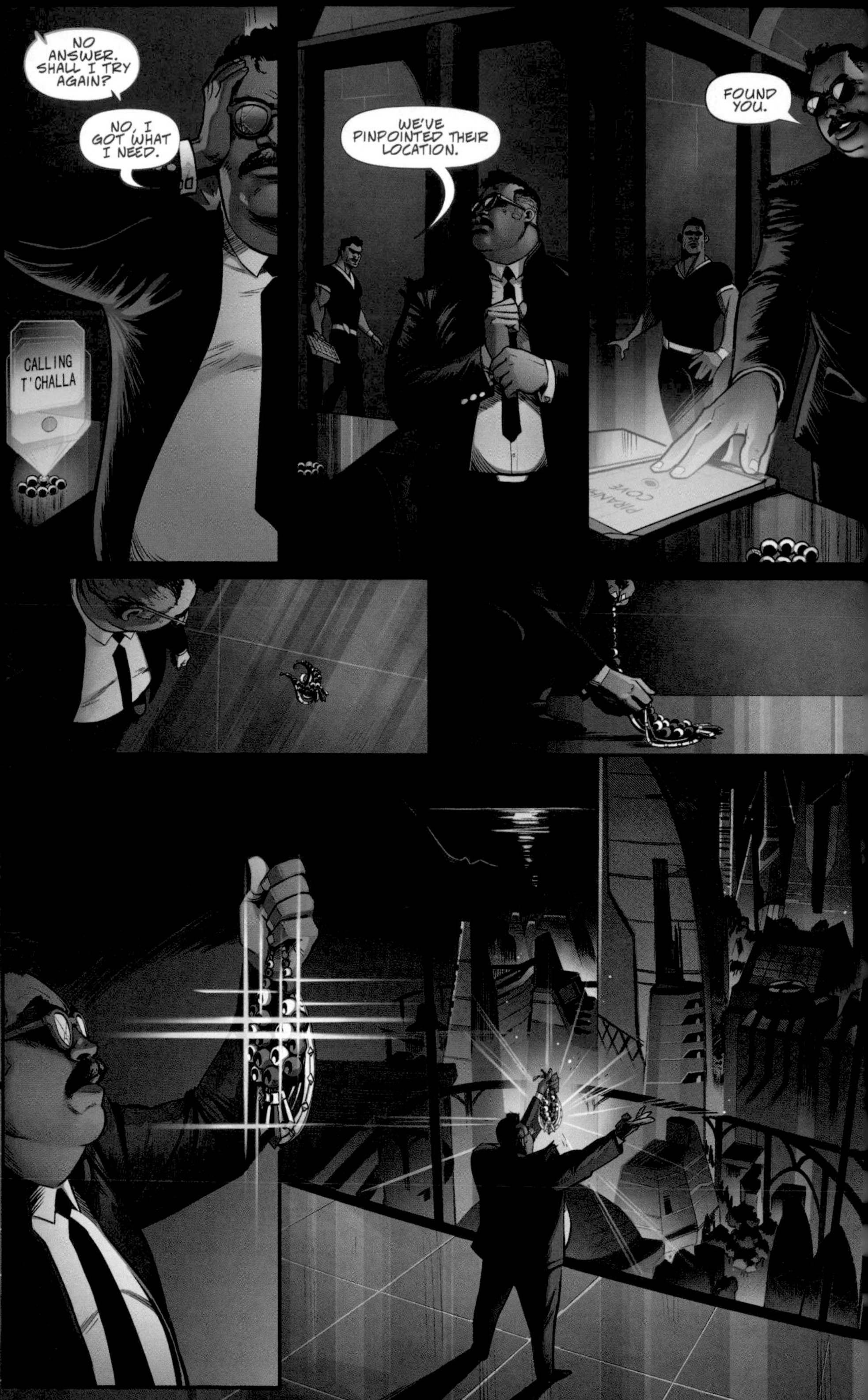
NO ANSWER. SHALL I TRY AGAIN?
NO, I GOT WHAT I NEED.
CALLING T'CHALLA
WE'VE PINPOINTED THEIR LOCATION.
FOUND YOU.

ART BY: KYLE BAKER

ART BY: JUAN SAMU
COLORS BY: DAVID GARCIA CRUZ

Piranha Cove, Wakanda.
AT LEAST WE'RE SAFE HERE.
HAVE YOU LOOKED DOWN LATELY?
I MEAN SAFE FROM THE HIPPO, ASHEI.
SHURI, DO YOU HAVE ANOTHER NANONET?
NO...
...SOMETHING BETTER.

YOU'VE BEEN USING A PROTON EXCAVATOR. THE U.N. BANNED THOSE YEARS AGO.
Wakanda. Beneath Mchezaji Tower.
BECAUSE YOU ELITES DON'T WANT THE CITIZENS TO SHARE IN YOUR WEALTH.
YOU WANT TO LIVE IN YOUR CASTLES EATING DIAMOND TRUFFLES OFF A PLATINUM CHANDELIER.
WELL, THAT AND THE TORNADOES.
I'M PRETTY SURE THE BAN WAS MOSTLY ABOUT TORNADOES.
THE NEW ERA OF JUSTICE IS UPON US! I GOT A NEW HD 4K GAMING SYSTEM WITH QUAD SPEAKERS, SURROUND SOUND, VR, AND AR.
I'M ALSO BUILDING A ROLLERCOASTER IN MY BACKYARD.
SERIOUSLY?
IT'S TIME TO RETURN WAKANDA TO THE PEOPLE!
YOU'RE GOING TO DESTROY US ALL!
NOT ME. WAKANDA'S GREED IS WHAT WILL DESTROY ITS PEOPLE. THEIR LOVE OF CLOTHES AND TREATS AND JEWELS AND MOTORCYCLES.
MMM. MOTORCYCLES.
ALL THIS ABUNDANCE IS THANKS TO QUADRUPLED VIBRANIUM PRODUCTION.
AND MADE POSSIBLE BY ME.
AND IN DOING IT, YOU'RE TEARING WAKANDA APART!
INDEED! BETWEEN THE TORNADOES, THE HEAT WAVE, AND THE MALARIA OUTBREAK...
...THESE MATERIAL THINGS ARE ALL THAT'S KEEPING WAKANDANS FROM TURNING ON THEIR INEPT ROYAL FAMILY.
AND TURNING TO THE MAN WHO MADE THEM RICH.

I CAN'T BELIEVE THAT WORKED. BUT WHY DIDN'T YOU DO THAT WHEN WE BAILED OUT OF THE AIRSHIP?
MY WINGS ARE A MODERN MARVEL, BUT EVEN THEY WOULDN'T SUPPORT THE WEIGHT OF THE SEATS WE WERE STRAPPED TO. ESPECIALLY AT THAT HEIGHT.
COMPUTER-- WHERE IS THE SHIP?
CALCULATING... DUE NORTH 500 METERS.
IN TWO METERS, TURN LEFT AND PROCEED 60 MET--ZZZT
COMPUTER? COMPUTER?
I THINK MY BATTERIES ARE DRAINED. ANYBODY?
SAME.
MINE, TOO.
WELL, AT LEAST WE WON'T HAVE TO LISTEN TO SHURI'S MUSIC.
OOPS!
WHAT HAPPENED, ASHEI?
I'M FINE. TRIPPED OVER A LOG.
THAT'S NO LOG.

EEEEEE!
SHHH! YOU'LL WAKE IT.
IT IS AWAKE!
THEY SLEEP WITH THEIR EYES OPEN. DON'T WORRY. IT'S NOT HUNGRY.
HOW DO YOU KNOW?
IT ALREADY ATE.
THERE'S THE SHIP!
THANK HEAVEN. A PYTHON-FREE ZONE.

HANDPRINT AUTHENTICATED. WELCOME BACK, SHURI.
THANK GOODNESS! THE DRUMS ARE INTACT.
A COUPLE OF THE CONNECTORS GOT SMASHED, AND THE GENERATOR'S RUPTURED, BUT I CAN FIX IT AND GET EVERYTHING RUNNING AGAIN. PROBABLY A FEW MINUTES...
A few minutes later.
I REPLACED SOME WIRE AND CIRCUITRY AND THE GENERATOR. THE MOSQUITO TRAP IS READY TO GO!
THE SHIP'S NOW FLYABLE, TOO, ASHEI, SO PREP FOR A FLIGHT TO THE HOSPITAL TO DELIVER THE CURE AND VACCINE.
YOU WON'T BE NEEDING THAT.
I'M NOT TAKING OFF THIS PARACHUTE. THERE MAY BE OTHER CLIFFS.
HM. DO WE HAVE ANY MORE?

HM. IT'S TOO QUIET.
WHO SLEEPS IN THEIR BOOTS?
THEY'VE ESCAPED!
MCHEZAJI IS GOING TO KILL ME!
WHAT ABOUT US?

OF COURSE THEY'RE ESCAPING. I'M SURROUNDED BY INCOMPETENTS.
BETTER SET MY BACKUP PLAN INTO MOTION...

OKAY, I CONNECTED THE ATOMIZER INTAKE TO THE BAIT BARREL.
WOW, THAT'S FOUL. I THINK IT'S GONE RANCID.
RANCID WOULD BE AN IMPROVEMENT.
SHURI, SHOULDN'T WE PUT THE BAIT CLOSER TO THE WATER? MOSQUITOES LOVE WATER.
WE'RE CLOSE ENOUGH. WE WANT TO BE THE BIGGEST TEMPTATION FOR MILES.
IS THAT THE REAL REASON?
DO I TELL YOU HOW TO DO *YOUR* JOB?
DAILY.
I'M JUST SAYING, IF YOU DON'T FEEL... COMFORTABLE, I COULD BRING THE MACHINE DOWN TO THE BAY FOR YOU. YOU COULD STAY UP HERE.
I CAN DO THIS. LIVES ARE AT STAKE.

Soon.
OKAY! POWER ON! NOW WE JUST NEED THEM TO TAKE THE BAIT!
SEE THOSE BLACK CLOUDS?
RAIN COMING. THAT'S ALL WE NEED RIGHT NOW.
DON'T WORRY. NOT WITH THIS DROUGHT.
THOSE AREN'T RAIN CLOUDS. BETTER TURN ON THE BUG ZAPPER!

ZAP
OKAY, WE'LL LET THE MACHINE DO ITS WORK.
EVERY MOSQUITO IN WAKANDA SHOULD BE DEAD IN 24 HOURS.
THAT IS QUITE A FUNK, EVEN THROUGH THE MASK.
I THINK WE LEFT ONE OF THOSE CARDBOARD PINE TREES HANGING IN THE COCKPIT. I'LL GO FIND IT.
RAAARRR!
H'RHAM! WHAT HAPPENED TO YOU?

OOF!
SHURI! STOP THE VACCINE! IT'S HEADING INTO THE COVE!
PIRANHA COVE...
...
WHAM
SPLASSH
NO!

WE'LL NEED REINFORCEMENTS. WHAT A TIME FOR T'CHALLA AND SHURI TO BE AWAY.
AND AT PIRANHA COVE, NO LESS.
WHAT'S THE STORY WITH SHURI AND PIRANHA COVE, ANYWAY? NOBODY WILL TALK ABOUT IT.
SHE WAS 11 YEARS OLD. CAMPING WITH HER SCOUT TROOP.
"AFTER THE ADULTS THOUGHT THEY WERE ASLEEP, SHURI AND SOME FRIENDS DECIDED TO GO EXPLORING.
"THEY THOUGHT THEY WERE OLD ENOUGH AND DIDN'T NEED ANYONE BOSSING THEM AROUND."
AND THEN?
...
SHURI KEPT INSISTING SHE KNEW BEST, THAT PIRANHAS ONLY EXISTED IN THE AMAZON AND THAT EVERYTHING WAS SAFE.
BUT SOMEBODY HAD PUT SOME PIRANHAS THERE, AND SOME OF HER FRIENDS GOT HURT. SHE FELT RESPONSIBLE.
HOW UNFORTUNATE.

BONK
ARGH!
GRRR...
WHACK
GAAAH!

WHERE AM I...?
IT'S OVERLOADING!
WHA-BOOM
HE'S UNCONSCIOUS, BUT VITAL SIGNS ARE STEADY.
H'RHAM, TOO.

OKAY. THINK, SHURI. I FROZE. THE VACCINE IS GONE, BUT THE CURE IS FINE. T'CHALLA IS HURT, BUT HE'LL BE FINE.
THOUSANDS OF PLAGUE-BEARING MOSQUITOES ARE STILL ALIVE AND HEADING DIRECTLY AT US--LESS FINE--AND THEY'LL BE HERE IN TWO MINUTES!
THE FIRST ONES ALREADY ARE...
GOTCHA.
SLAP
THAT WAS A MALE. THEY DON'T DRINK BLOOD.
WELL, THAT MALE SHOULD HAVE RESPECTED MY PERSONAL SPACE. HOW DID YOU KNOW IT WAS MALE, ANYWAY?
FEMALES ARE BIGGER. AND THEY... *BITE*.
WAIT, THAT GIVES ME AN IDEA.
I'M GOING TO NEED YOU TO REPLACE THE LID ON THIS BAIT BARREL AS SOON AS I GET OUT.
GET T'CHALLA, H'RHAM, AND THIS BARREL ON THE SHIP AND WAIT FOR ME WITH THE ENGINE RUNNING.
UGH!
I'VE GOT SOME FISH TO FEED.

SHURI...
I GUESS WE'LL LET YOU ABOARD. THAT BATH MUST HAVE HELPED WITH YOUR STENCH.
THAT'S WHY WE BROUGHT THE BAIT BARREL. GOTTA LURE THE SURVIVING BUGS AWAY FROM THE WATER.
WHY ON EARTH...?
BECAUSE, DEAR BROTHER, I JUST TURNED A SWARM OF BLOODSUCKERS INTO THOUSANDS OF TINY SYRINGES FULL OF MALARIA VACCINE!
NOW LET'S GET THIS MEDICINE TO THE HOSPITAL TO CURE THE ONES ALREADY AFFECTED.

HELLO, MOTHER. THE CURE WAS DELIVERED, AND THE VACCINE IS BEING... DISTRIBUTED SO OTHERS WON'T BE INFECTED.
I'LL BE SO GLAD WHEN THIS IS OVER.
IT'S ABOUT TO BE ALL OVER FOR YOU, T'CHALLA!
MCHEZAJI? WHERE IS MY MOTHER?
I'VE GOT GOOD NEWS AND BAD NEWS, T'CHALLA. THE GOOD NEWS IS VIBRANIUM PRODUCTION WILL QUADRUPLE--AGAIN.
THE BAD NEWS IS IT'S GOING TO DESTROY WAKANDA.
I WILL STOP YOU.

"I'VE ALWAYS WANTED A LEVER-ACTIVATED WORLD DESTRUCTION MACHINE."
BEFORE THESE PROTON EXCAVATORS COULD BE OUTLAWED, THEY FIRST HAD TO BE BUILT AND IN USE.
AFTER THEY WERE FORBIDDEN, ONLY THE UPPER TIER OF POLITICAL POWER HAD BIOMETRIC SECURITY ACCESS.
MY QUEEN, MAY I TAKE YOUR HAND?
COME AND GET IT.
WHAP
BEEP
OH, T'CHALLA. I SO WISH YOU COULD BE HERE TO WATCH THIS.

YOUR WISH HAS BEEN GRANTED.
UNHFF!
POW
OH, YEAH. HIS HEAD COMES OFF. I SHOULD HAVE MENTIONED THAT.
HUH. THANKS FOR THE HEADS-UP.
SLAM
AGGH!
BEHOLD! FIVE DEADLY TORNADOES ARE FORMING!
YOU SHALL BE EXTINGUISHED BY THE VERY AIR YOU BREATHE! AND I, KING CADAVER, WILL RULE OVER WHAT'S LEFT OF HUMANITY!
YOU FOOL! ULTIMATE VICTORY SHALL BE MINE!

YOU SHOULD HAVE QUIT WHILE YOU WERE A HEAD.
I'M THE ONLY KING IN WAKANDA.
WHOOSH
AAAEEEE!
SEE WHAT HAPPENS WHEN YOU DON'T PICK UP MY CALLS?
I'LL TELL YOU A SECRET, MOTHER. I ALWAYS LISTEN. I PROMISED MY FATHER I WOULD ALWAYS PROTECT YOU. AND WAKANDA.
SO WHO'S GOING TO TELL THE PEOPLE THEY HAVE TO GIVE BACK ALL THE ROLLERCOASTERS AND VIDEO GAMES?
THEY'LL NEED THOSE WHILE THINGS SLOWLY GO BACK TO NORMAL.
"ESPECIALLY THE VIDEO GAMES. WE DON'T NEED TO START RIOTS."
The End.

ART BY: MICHAEL AVON OEMING

ART BY: GABRIEL RODRIGUEZ
COLORS BY: NELSON DÁNIEL

ART BY: ALEX MILNE
COLORS BY: PARIS ALLEYNE

MARVEL

MARVEL ACTION

BLACK PANTHER

STORMY WEATHER